SUBWAY SPARROW

SUBWAY SPARROW

Leyla Torres

SQUARE
FISH
Farrar · Straus · Giroux

At the Atlantic Avenue station in Brooklyn, a sparrow flew into a subway car on the D train.

"Little bird, what are you doing down here?"

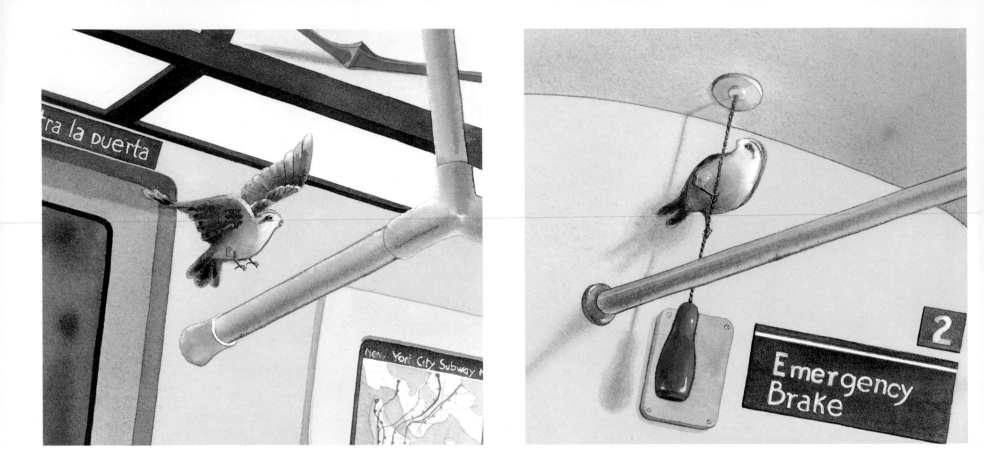

With a rumble, the train began to move.

"It's okay, it's okay—don't be afraid. I want to help you."

"¿Y esto? ¡Un pajarito en el metro!"

"Mister, maybe you can catch him with your
hat…"
"Sí, con mi sombrero tal vez lo atajemos."

"If I go that way, maybe he'll fly toward you."
"Sí, ¡corre! ¡corre!"
The train rocked back and forth as it gained speed.

"Hey, there's a bird in here!"

"I'll help, but my hands are so big, I might hurt him."

"¡Ay, se nos voló otra vez!"

"Oh no, he's off again!"

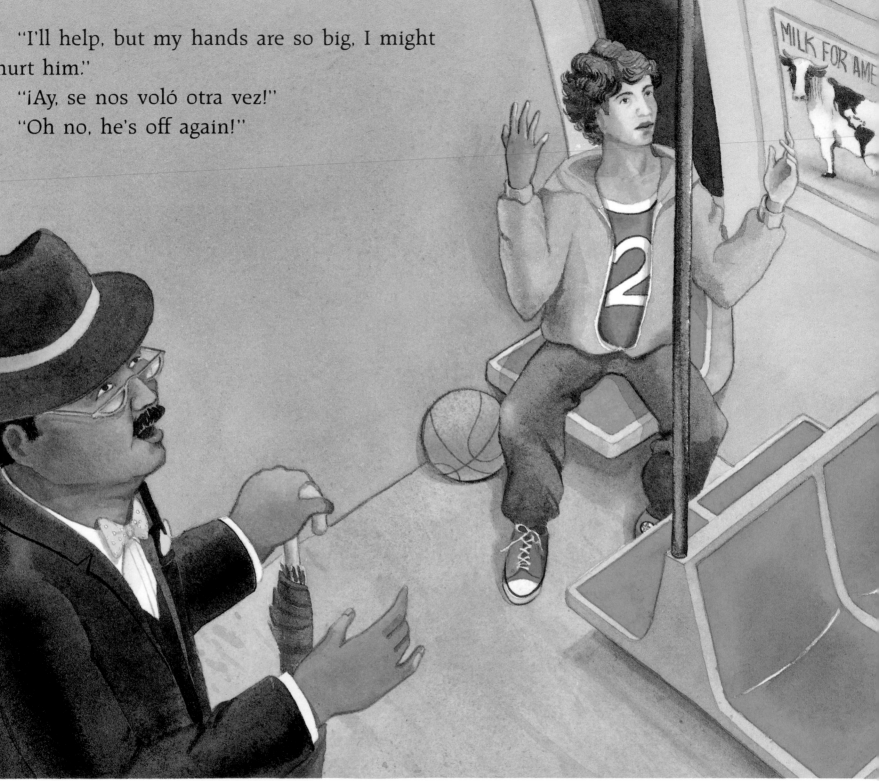

"O jejku, co ty wróbelku robisz w pociągu?"

"We're slowing down! Let's catch him before
the crowd gets on the train."

"Quizá con mi sombrilla."

"Nie dotykaj go parasolem!"

"No, forget the umbrella—it might hurt him."

"Moja apaszka."
"Yeah, cover him with the scarf!"
"Sí, cubrámoslo."
"Hurry, I'll pick him up."

The doors of the subway car closed. With a hiss, the train pulled away from the platform.

"His heart is beating so quickly ... He's so
soft, like a little cloud in my hands."

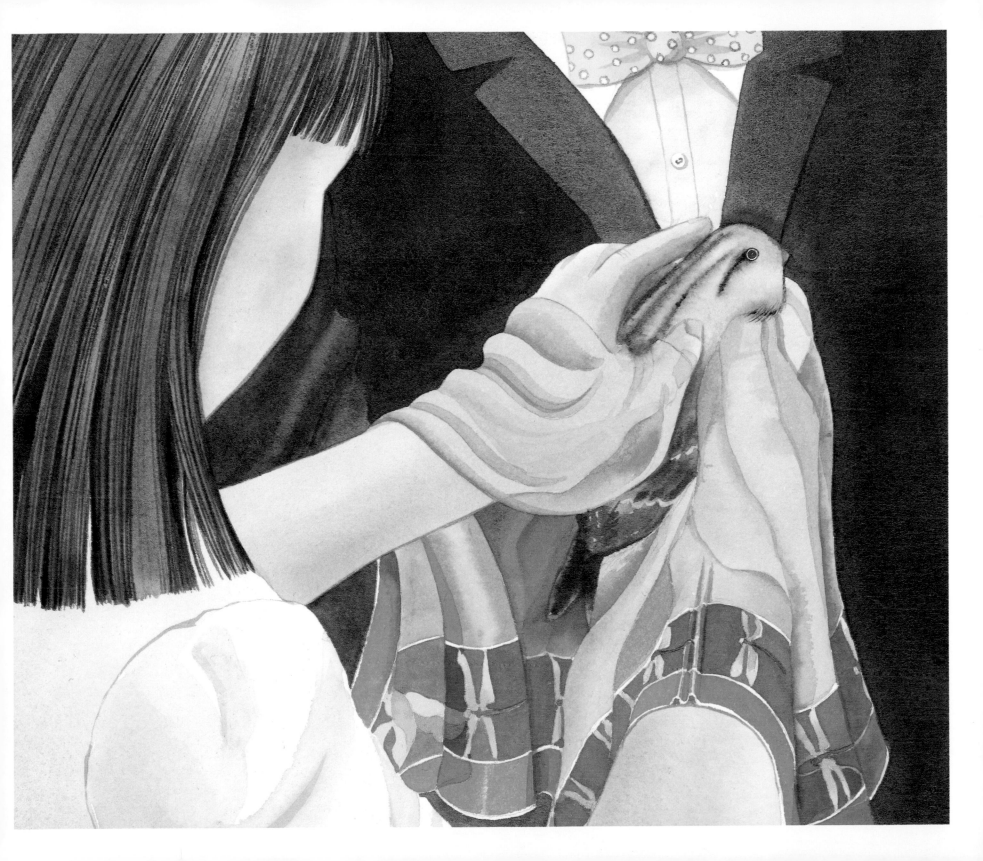

"Adios, pajarito."
"Good luck!"
"Do widzenia."
"Bye, little one."

For Juan

SQUARE
FISH

An Imprint of Macmillan

Library of Congress catalog card number: 97-55104
ISBN 978-0-374-47129-3

Originally published in the United States by Farrar Straus Giroux
Published in Canada by HarperCollins Canada Ltd
First Square Fish Edition: March 2012
Square Fish logo designed by Filomena Tuosto
Book designed by Martha Rago
mackids.com

17 19 20 18

AR: 1.6